Cub's First Summer

by Rebecca Elliott

D0453077

Published by Top That! Publishing plc
Tide Mill Way, Woodbridge, Suffolk, IP12 1AP, UK
www.topthatpublishing.com
Text and illustrations copyright © 2012 Rebecca Elliott.

All rights reserved
0 2 4 6 8 9 7 5 3 1
Printed and bound in China

Creative Director – Simon Couchman
Editorial Director – Daniel Graham

Written and illustrated by Rebecca Elliott

All rights reserved. No part of this publication may be reproduced, stored in a retrieval system, or transmitted in any form or by any means, electronic, mechanical, photocopying, recording or otherwise, without the prior written permission of the publisher. Neither this book nor any part or any of the illustrations, photographs or reproductions contained in it shall be sold or disposed of otherwise than as a complete book, and any unauthorised sale of such part illustration, photograph or reproduction shall be deemed to be a breach of the publisher's copyright.

ISBN 978-1-78244-016-1

A catalogue record for this book is available from the British Library
Printed and bound in China

'For my little cubs – Clemmie and Toby. x'

It was the first day of summer and Cub had just woken up. 'Good morning,' said Mum. 'Let's go and explore the forest. Come on ...'

'Why is it so hot?'
asked Cub.

'So that we can splash in the cool water!' giggled Mum.

And the sun shone down.

'Why are the crickets so loud?' asked Cub.

'Because they want us to
jump high like them!'
exclaimed Mum.

And the sun grew hazy.

'Why are the days so long?' asked Cub.

'So that we have more time for fun!' laughed Mum.

And the sunlight began to fade.

'Why are there so many flowers?' asked Cub.
'So that we can enjoy their beautiful smell!' sniffed Mum.

And clouds began
to gather in the sky.

'Why are the birds singing so loudly?' asked Cub.

'So that we can dance to their music!' sang Mum.

And the clouds got darker.

'Why are the bees so busy?' asked Cub.
'Because they want to make us lots of yummy honey!' said Mum.

And the air
grew heavy.

'Why are the vegetables so big?' asked Cub.

'So that we can feast on them!' spluttered Mum,
with her mouth full of carrot.
And the first flash of lightning lit up the sky.

'What's that noise?' asked Cub, as the first rumble of thunder grumbled all around him.

'Oh no!' gasped Mum.
'Quick! Follow me before the thunderstorm gets worse!'

And back they went through the vegetable patch, past the trees, back and forth through the meadow, and over the river until, at last, they found their way home!

'Why is the thunderstorm so scary?' asked Cub.

'So that we can
snuggle up tight,'
whispered Mum,
with a smile.

'Why am I so tired?' yawned Cub.
'Because it is sleepy time,' murmured Mum.
'Night night, little cub.'